# The StinkySneakers Mystery

## Beverly Lewis

# Beverly Lewis Books for Young Readers

## PICTURE BOOKS

*Annika's Secret Wish*
*Cows in the House*
*Just Like Mama*

## THE CUL-DE-SAC KIDS

*The Double Dabble Surprise*
*The Chicken Pox Panic*
*The Crazy Christmas Angel Mystery*
*No Grown-ups Allowed*
*Frog Power*
*The Mystery of Case D. Luc*
*The Stinky Sneakers Mystery*
*Pickle Pizza*
*Mailbox Mania*
*The Mudhole Mystery*
*Fiddlesticks*
*The Crabby Cat Caper*
*Tarantula Toes*
*Green Gravy*
*Backyard Bandit Mystery*
*Tree House Trouble*
*The Creepy Sleep-Over*
*The Great TV Turn-Off*
*Piggy Party*
*The Granny Game*
*Mystery Mutt*
*Big Bad Beans*
*The Upside-Down Day*
*The Midnight Mystery*

*Katie and Jake and the Haircut Mistake*

www.BeverlyLewis.com

# THE CUL-DE-SAC KIDS

# The Stinky Sneakers Mystery

Beverly Lewis

## BETHANY HOUSE PUBLISHERS

MINNEAPOLIS, MINNESOTA 55438

*The Stinky Sneakers Mystery*
Copyright © 1996
Beverly Lewis

Cover illustration by Paul Turnbaugh
Story illustrations by Janet Huntington

Published by Bethany House Publishers
11400 Hampshire Avenue South
Bloomington, Minnesota 55438

Bethany House Publishers is a division of
Baker Publishing Group, Grand Rapids, Michigan.

Printed in the United States of America

**Library of Congress Cataloging-in-Publication Data**

Lewis, Beverly, 1949–
    The stinky sneakers mystery / by Beverly Lewis
       p.  cm. — (Cul-de-sac kids ; 7)
    Summary: Jason is sure his science project will win first prize, until he finds out what the other Cul-de-sac Kids are planning.

    [1. Science projects—Fiction.] I. Title. II. Series:
Lewis, Beverly, 1949–      Cul-de-sac kids ; 7.
PZ7.L58464Ss     1996
[Fic]—dc20                         96–4439
ISBN 1–55661–727–5 (pbk.)        CIP
                                         AC

To
Darrel Barnes
(Surprise!)

THE CUL-DE-SAC KIDS

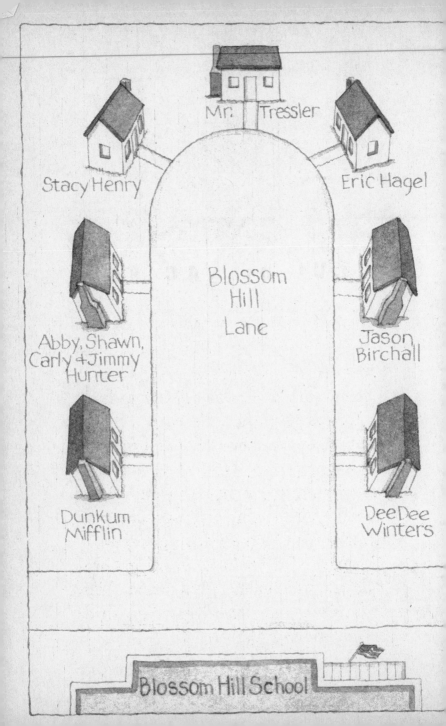

Mr. Tressler

Stacy Henry

Eric Hagel

Blossom
Hill
Lane

Abby, Shawn,
Carly & Jimmy
Hunter

Jason
Birchall

Dunkum
Mifflin

DeeDee
Winters

Blossom Hill School

# ONE

Jason Birchall wanted first place in the science fair. So did *all* the kids in Miss Hershey's class.

But Jason was the only one bragging about his project.

He bragged to his friends Eric, Shawn, and Dunkum. He bragged during math, at lunch, and all during recess.

Jason was still talking about his project on the walk home from school. "I'm getting first place this year," he said. "Can you guess why?"

Eric Hagel and Shawn Hunter shook their heads. "Nope," said Eric.

"Nope," repeated Shawn. "I not." He was still learning English. Shawn and his brother, Jimmy, had come from Korea.

"Hurry up, Jason. Spit it out," Dunkum Mifflin said. "What's so great about your project?"

Jason spotted Abby Hunter and her best friend, Stacy Henry. "Hey, girls," he called to them. "Wanna hear about my science project?"

Abby and Stacy didn't even turn around. They whispered to each other instead.

*They're really dying to know*, thought Jason.

In the middle of the cul-de-sac, Jason stopped. He put his hands up to his mouth and shouted, "I have the best science project in the world!"

Abby glanced over her shoulder.

"You're going to make yourself disappear, right?"

Stacy Henry giggled.

Eric and Shawn tried not to.

"Very funny," said Jason.

"Come on," Dunkum said. "Give it to us straight. What's your project?"

"Yes, give us *good* hint," Shawn said.

Jason folded his arms across his chest. He looked at his cul-de-sac friends.

And . . . *whoosh!*

The words shot past his lips. Out into the air they flew. "Super sprouts," he said. "I'm growing super sprouts."

Eric laughed. "Anyone can do that."

"Not the way *I'm* growing them," Jason said.

"What's so special about it?" asked Dunkum.

Jason's voice got louder. "My sprouts are growing in a piece of carpet."

Shawn looked puzzled. "Magic sprouts?"

Eric's eyes got wide. But he was silent.

Shawn grinned at Jason. "You get first place!"

"You're right!" Jason shouted. "And next week we'll find out!"

"We sure will," Eric said. There was a sly grin on his face. A very sly grin.

Now Jason was worried. He watched Eric run up the steps to his house.

What was *Eric's* project? And why was he acting so strange?

# TWO

Jason was counting. Three more days until the science fair.

He sat on the beanbag in his room. He was trying to do math. Ten problems for tomorrow.

Jason groaned. He was only half finished.

He couldn't keep his mind on math. He gazed at the windowsill. The super sprouts were growing there in a piece of green carpet.

Jason stared at them. He stared hard.

He imagined a giant trophy floating over the sprouts.

Jason could hear Miss Hershey's voice. She was telling the class about his project. Miss Hershey was bragging about him.

"Now for the best student in the class," she said. "Will Jason Birchall please come forward?"

The kids were green with envy.

Abby and Stacy were pointing.

Eric and Dunkum were leaning forward in their seats.

Everyone was whispering. *Jason* . . . *Jason* . . . His name flew around the classroom.

Jason stood up and went to Miss Hershey's desk. All eyes were on him.

The teacher held up a shiny, gold trophy. First place!

"Wow," said the kids.

Jason held up his green carpet square

and the super sprouts. He held them high.

"Jason! Yippe-e-e!" The whole class cheered. Wild, happy cheering.

★　★　★

Z-z-z. Jason was asleep in his beanbag.

The phone rang. Jason jumped.

His mother called to him, "It's your friend Eric."

Jason rubbed his eyes. He pulled himself out of the beanbag. "I'm coming," he mumbled.

He shuffled down the hallway. His mother held out the phone.

"Hello?" Jason said.

"Hi," Eric said. "You know that sprout project of yours?"

Jason yawned. "Uh-huh."

"Well, don't plan on winning first place." Eric sounded too sure of himself.

"Why not?" Jason asked.

16

"Because there's no chance," Eric replied. "No chance you'll get first place."

Jason took off his glasses. He stared at them. "That's what *you* think!" he said and hung up the phone.

★   ★   ★

The next day was Tuesday. Eric was absent from school. He never missed!

Jason felt jumpy. He got that way when he didn't take his pills. Being an A.D.D. kid was hard. But the pills helped him think about his work.

Today was different. He'd taken his pills at breakfast, but he was still jumpy. Jason jittered. He twittered.

Something kept zipping around in his brain. He worried all through math and history. Through recess and lunch.

Eric Hagel was *never* sick. Why had he stayed home?

During afternoon recess, Dunkum shot baskets with Jason. "Stop worry-

17

ing," Dunkum said. "Eric's probably just sick."

"How do you know?" Jason asked.

Dunkum shrugged. "I don't."

Jason told him about Eric's sneaky smile. Then he told him about Eric's phone call. "He's acting weird," Jason said.

Dunkum only laughed. "Eric wouldn't stay home to do a science project. No way!"

Jason dribbled the ball. He aimed, shot, and missed. "Well, I think something's up."

Dunkum's turn. He shot and made it. "You'll see. There's probably nothing to worry about."

The bell rang.

Jason raced into the school building. Maybe Dunkum is right, he thought. Maybe there isn't anything to worry about.

He went to his desk and opened his

math book. But Jason couldn't get Eric's sly smile out of his mind.

"Jason," Miss Hershey called, "please come to the board."

Jason went. He tried not to look at Eric's empty desk.

Why had Eric stayed home?

What was *really* going on?

# THREE

The last bell rang.

Jason didn't walk home with the Cul-de-sac Kids. He ran straight to Eric's house. Right up to his front porch.

Eric's grandpa sat in a wicker chair. "Hello, Jason," Mr. Hagel said.

"How are you today?" Jason asked.

The old man chuckled. "Not too bad for my age."

Jason wondered, *Should I ask about Eric?*

Mr. Hagel peered over his newspaper.

"If you're looking for Eric, he's upstairs in bed."

Jason remembered what Dunkum had said. "Is . . . is Eric too sick for company?" he asked.

"My goodness, no." Mr. Hagel waved his hand. "Go wake him. He's sleeping the daylight away."

Jason wondered about that. "What's wrong with Eric?"

"Ah, nothing a good night's sleep won't cure."

"Sleep?" Jason said. "Eric's not sick?"

The old man shook his head. "My grandson is mighty busy these days. I think he was up half the night."

"Busy with science?" Jason asked.

Mr. Hagel chuckled. "That's right."

Jason opened the screen door and marched into Eric's house. Up the stairs and right into his friend's bedroom.

Eric was working at his desk. Still wearing pj's.

"Looks like you're not very sick," Jason said.

Eric leaped out of his chair. He stood in front of his desk. "What . . . what are you doing here?"

Jason inched closer, but Eric didn't move.

"I said, what are you doing here?"

Jason pushed up his glasses. "Your grandpa told me to wake you."

Eric shook his head. "I don't believe you."

"Go and ask," Jason said.

"It's a trick," Eric said. "You just want to see my science project."

"You're wrong, Eric." Jason turned to go.

"You think you're so smart," Eric kept talking. "But, Jason Birchall, you just wait!"

Jason wanted to bop his friend. He

really wanted to. But he made a fist inside his pocket and punched it into his pants. Then he headed for the steps.

"No, *you* wait," Jason muttered.

# FOUR

It was Wednesday.

One more day till the science fair began.

Miss Hershey's class was ready. Especially Jason.

At recess he started bragging again. "*My* project will take first place."

Eric sat on a swing. He pushed his foot into the sand. He was never like this. Too quiet.

Jason wondered why.

Dunkum and Shawn came over.

"What's up?" Dunkum asked.

Jason said, "Eric's not talking."

Dunkum laughed. "Why not?"

Shawn spoke up. "Maybe still sick?"

Jason shouted, "He was never sick!"

Jason paced back and forth in the sand. He wondered why Eric was keeping his project a secret. It worried him.

Abby and Stacy came over. They wanted to swing.

Eric got off and went to play ball. Dunkum and Shawn left, too.

Jason started to leave. Then he heard Abby tell Stacy about her project.

"I can make it rain," Abby said.

Stacy giggled. "Sounds drippy."

Jason hung around. Abby's project sounded terrific.

Abby laughed with her best friend. "It's simple. All you need is an ice-cold soup dipper and a teapot."

Jason couldn't believe his ears. Where did Abby get such a good idea?

Then Stacy told Abby about *her* project. Jason crept closer.

"My project is called A Tight Squeeze," said Stacy. "I'm going to show how to make a giant hole out of paper."

"Sounds easy." Abby began to swing.

"Big enough to put over your head? Oh, and the paper can't rip while you do it," Stacy explained.

Abby stopped swinging. "Now *that* sounds hard."

"Sure does," Jason said.

The girls looked up. "You were snooping!" Abby said.

Jason grinned.

"By the way, how are your super sprouts doing?" Abby asked.

Jason stood tall. He stuck out his chest. "My sprouts are super and they're sprouting. That's how they're doing."

The girls giggled. "What a silly project," Stacy said.

"Is not!" Jason replied.

They began to chant. "Jason's growing super sprouts . . . super sprouts . . . super sprouts."

Then they started giggling again.

Jason couldn't stand it. He ran to the ball field.

The girls had no right to make fun of his sprouts.

Super or not.

# FIVE

On the way home from school, Dunkum told about his science project. "I'm doing a taste test."

"You're going to feed us?" Jason said.

Dunkum nodded. "Just some turnips, carrots, and an apple."

"Sounds yucky," Jason said.

"Bet you can't tell the difference between them," Dunkum said.

"Bet I can," Jason said. "Easy!"

Dunkum's eyebrows shot up. "We'll see."

Shawn nodded. "Dunkum have super tongue."

Dunkum chuckled.

But Eric was silent.

"What about *your* project?" Jason asked Shawn.

"I make you see sound," he said. "I make sound dance on wall."

"Are you joking?" Jason asked. "You can't do that!"

Shawn's dark eyes were shining. "You will see."

"Tomorrow," Dunkum said.

"Tomorrow!" Jason shouted. But he was thinking about *his* project. Not Shawn's.

Jason dashed home to check his sprouts.

His mother was waiting at the door. "Time for a snack." She gave him a hug.

Jason took his afternoon pill with his snack. Then he ran to his room.

Sunshine poured onto the windowsill.

He hurried over to his super sprouts. Bright green.

Next he touched the long carpet square. Damp.

Jason grinned. He found his notebook and wrote down the steps.

1. Shallow box
2. Plastic trash bag lining
3. Scrap of carpet
4. Alfalfa seeds
5. Some sunshine
6. Water
7. And . . . super sprouts!

He signed his name to the science paper. Everything was ready.

Jason went outside to ride his bike.

Eric was across the street at Dunkum's house. He was carrying a folder. A large black one.

When Jason got back from his ride, Eric was coming out of Abby and Shawn's house. What was he doing?

Jason zipped down the street, pretending not to care. He rode to the school playground and hid behind a tree. He spied as Eric headed to Stacy's house.

Eric rang the doorbell, and Stacy let him in.

*This is weird*, thought Jason. *Eric is up to something. Something very strange!*

# SIX

*Snooping on Eric is great!* thought Jason.

He watched Eric go to Mr. Tressler's house next. Mr. Tressler and Eric's grandpa were good friends.

Eric rang the doorbell and waited. Mr. Tressler let him in.

Jason waited, still hiding behind the tree.

Soon, Eric came out. He headed to Jason's house next.

Quickly, Jason hopped on his bike. He

had to know what Eric was doing!

Jason flew down Blossom Hill Lane. He braked in front of his house.

Eric stopped on Jason's driveway and frowned.

"What's up?" Jason asked.

"Can I borrow your thumb?" Eric asked.

"My thumb?" Jason said. "What for?"

Eric smiled. "For my science project."

Jason got off his bike. He folded his arms across his chest. "I'm not helping *you*. And that's final."

"But—"

"You heard me!" Jason shouted. And he stomped into the house.

★ ★ ★

Thirty minutes later, Jason's doorbell rang. He was ready to sock Eric in the nose.

Jason grabbed the doorknob.

It was Stacy Henry. She was holding

her white cockapoo puppy. His name was Sunday Funnies—because he always found the Sunday comics first. Before anyone!

Stacy's science folder was tucked under her arm. "I need to test my project," she said. "Can you help me?"

Jason didn't want to at first. Why was everyone asking for his help?

"Please?" Stacy said. "It won't take long."

He opened the screen door. "Okay."

They went into the kitchen. Stacy put her puppy down on the floor. She took out a piece of paper and some scissors from her folder.

"Here," she said. "Try to cut a hole big enough to pass over your body."

Jason picked up the scissors. "Easy."

While he cut, Stacy asked about his project. "Can I see your super sprouts?"

"Only if you don't laugh at them," he

said. He put the paper and scissors on the table.

"I promise."

"Okay then," Jason said.

He went to his room and came right back, carrying the box. Inside, the carpet was full of bushy green sprouts.

She sniffed the sprouts. "Smells good. May I taste?"

"Just a little," Jason said. "I need lots of them for tomorrow."

Stacy pulled off a tiny sprig and put it in her mouth. "Mm-m, good!"

Sunday Funnies stood up on his hind legs.

Stacy laughed. "Look, my dog wants a bite too."

"I can't let a dog eat my first prize!"

"Aw, just a little?" Stacy pleaded.

The puppy was still begging.

Jason refused to look at Stacy's dog. "How long is he going to do that?"

"Till he gets what he wants," she said.

Jason frowned. He looked at Sunday Funnies. "Oh, all right. Give him a taste."

Sunday Funnies ate the sprouts, then he licked his chops.

"He loves them!" Stacy exclaimed.

"I was afraid of that," Jason said. He picked up the paper and scissors and began to cut.

Stacy watched him. "Can you do it? Can you make a hole fit over your head?" she asked.

He slid the circle halfway over his head. It was too small to go farther.

Stacy said, "I think you're stuck."

Jason pulled the paper off his head. "This is impossible."

"Here, I'll show you how," Stacy said.

Sunday Funnies was begging again. Jason noticed it. "Put my sprouts away," he said. He pointed to the top of the refrigerator.

Stacy stood on a chair and put the box up there. Now the sprouts were safe.

When Stacy got down, she took another piece of paper and folded it in half—long, like a hot dog. She made thirteen cuts on the folded paper.

Jason watched carefully.

Gently, she stretched the paper out. And climbed through.

"Wow, that's cool!" Jason said. But he didn't really mean it. Stacy's project was too good.

Stacy picked up her folder, scissors, and paper. She walked to the front door. Sunday Funnies followed.

"Thanks for your help," she said.

Jason closed the door without saying a word.

# SEVEN

Jason yawned. He opened his eyes.
Thursday at last!

He flew down the hall to the bathroom and washed his face. He got dressed in record time.

At breakfast, Jason took his pill without a fuss. And he ate everything on his plate.

"This is a very big day," his father said.

"Sure is," his mother said.

"My sprouts are super!" Jason said.

43

"They're the very best!"

His parents smiled at him across the table.

Jason looked at his watch. "It's too early for school."

"You could start gathering up your things," his mother suggested.

His father patted him on the back. "Have a great science fair," he said and left for work.

His mother went to take her shower.

Jason scampered to his room and found his notebook. He'd been counting the hours. The fair started today. It would end tomorrow with the judging.

He couldn't wait.

Then Jason remembered Stacy's paper hole project, and Abby's homemade rain.

Shawn was going to make sound dance on the wall. Dunkum had a turnip taste test.

But what about Eric? What was *he* doing?

Quickly, Jason went to the window-sill. Time to take his super sprouts to school. But . . .

The sprouts were gone!

"Where's my project?"

He searched his room. Then he ran through the house. But his sprouts were nowhere to be seen.

Gone!

"Where are they?" he wailed.

He called to his mother through the bathroom door.

She didn't answer.

Jason pounded on the door. "Mom!"

"I'm in the shower," she called back. "I can't hear you."

Jason stood in the middle of the living room. He shook with worry. *What can I do?*

A huge lump crowded his throat.

Then he heard sounds outside. Running to the window, he looked out.

The Cul-de-sac Kids were walking to school together. They bunched up in front of his house. Waiting.

Jason opened the front door. "Wait a minute," he called.

He couldn't tell them about his missing sprouts. After all his bragging, he just couldn't!

Jason ran around the house searching for something. Anything. What could he use for a science project?

He looked under his bed and found some dirty socks. Yuk! He held his nose.

He thought of Shawn's project—making sound dance on the wall. Maybe he could make smells dance, too.

No. That was silly.

He ran to the window. The kids were still waiting—with their science projects.

"Hurry up!" Abby called from the street.

Jason banged into the kitchen. He looked around for something to take for the science fair. But there was nothing. Nothing!

*So much for first place*, he thought.

Miss Hershey would give him a big, fat zero!

# EIGHT

Jason heard a knock on the screen door.

"Come in," he said.

In came the Cul-de-sac Kids.

Abby and Stacy.

Dunkum, Shawn, and Shawn's little brother, Jimmy. Abby's little sister, Carly, with her best friend, Dee Dee Winters.

And Eric.

"Where's your science project?" Abby asked.

49

Jason was speechless.

"Yeah, let's see those super sprouts," Eric said.

"I . . . uh . . ." Jason knew they would laugh. He couldn't tell them.

Stacy looked at her watch. "We better get going. We don't want to be late."

The kids were too excited to wait for Jason. They left for school. Without him.

Jason decided to look outside for his sprouts. He went around the side of the house.

He sniffed the air. He coughed. Something smelled rotten, like three-week-old gym socks!

Eric's grandpa was sitting on the porch next door. "Good morning, Jason," he said.

Jason stepped closer. "What's that smell?"

Mr. Hagel was spreading cheese on some bread. "This, young man, is my favorite cheese. It's called Limburger."

Jason pinched his nose shut. "Smells horrible!"

Mr. Hagel grinned. "Ah, but the taste is out of this world. Care for some?"

"I . . . uh . . . better not." Jason stepped back, away from the odor.

"Just try it," Mr. Hagel said. "Have it in your lunch, maybe." He wrapped a lump of it in plastic and gave it to Jason.

"Uh . . . thanks." Jason stuffed the nasty-smelling cheese into his pocket. He would toss it in the trash later.

★ ★ ★

At school, the kids were lining up outside. Their hands were filled with science projects.

Jason got in line. He hid his hands in his pants pockets.

Eric teased, "Hey, Sprout Man, tell the truth. You didn't really make a project, did you?"

Jason felt his neck get hot. "You're

wrong!" He ran up to Eric.

Stacy and Abby pushed the boys apart. "Stop it!" Stacy yelled. "I saw Jason's sprouts yesterday."

Eric looked surprised. "Oh, really? Well, where are they now?"

"Disappeared," Jason muttered. "They're missing."

Shawn frowned. "Missing from earth?"

"No, from Jason's house," Abby explained.

"Too bad," Shawn said. "I want to see super sprouts."

Eric snickered. "You're not the only one!"

Jason stuffed his hands into his pockets again. His fingers bumped the mound of smelly cheese. Eric's grandpa's cheese.

And suddenly, he had a great idea.

# NINE

The mats were out in P.E. It was tumbling day.

Jason and the rest of the class lined their shoes up along the wall.

Then they warmed up with three forward rolls each. Next came three backward rolls. Some kids did handstands.

Jason took off his glasses and did two backflips with help. Dunkum did a handstand for five seconds.

Eric stood on his head without wobbling. Shawn practiced walking on his hands.

Abby and Stacy did double cart-wheels.

*Whew!* Jason's mouth was getting dry. He needed a long, cold drink.

So did Eric. And Dunkum.

The teacher let Jason go first. Then Eric. They were only allowed to go one at a time.

Eric came back from the water fountain. "Mr. Sprout Man gets a zero," he teased.

"Leave me alone," Jason shot back.

Eric scrunched up his face. "How could you lose a science project? That's dumb."

Jason was boiling mad. He needed another drink. The teacher said he could have one more.

Hurrying toward the drinking fountain, Jason passed the row of sneakers. He spotted Abby's red and blue ones.

He saw Shawn's blue sneakers.

*Here's my chance*, he thought. And he

dug into his pocket and pulled out the smelly cheese.

After class, the teacher blew her whistle twice. Time to get shoes back on.

Quickly, Jason found his sneakers.

He heard Abby squeal, "This is so yucky!"

"Gross!" Eric said.

"Pee-uwee!" Stacy shouted.

Jason jumped up. "What's that smell?" He pinched his nose shut.

"Very big stink," Shawn said. He pushed his foot into his sneaker. His eyes bugged out. "Something feel mushy inside." Shawn yanked his foot out.

Abby came over to see. "Yuk!" she said. "You've got rotten cheese in there, too."

"So do I," Eric hollered.

"Me too," called Stacy.

"Me three," said Abby. "Who *did* this?"

Eric shook his sneakers out. "Smells

like Grandpa's cheese!"

Abby's eyebrows flew up. "Why'd you put your grandpa's cheese in our sneakers?"

"I'd never do that!" Eric held up his own pair of sneakers, shaking his head.

By now, Miss Hershey was waiting in the hall. "Time to line up," she called.

"I'm not wearing these sneakers anymore," Abby told Eric.

Stacy, Shawn, and Eric agreed. They went to class in their socks.

Jason followed, holding his nose.

Abby got in line. "My sneakers are ruined," she said. "I can't believe Eric did this!"

Eric pushed ahead in line. "I told you, I *didn't* do it!"

"Right," Abby said. "And I don't believe you."

Jason didn't smile. He didn't laugh. But he wanted to—right in Eric's face.

*Serves him right*, he thought.

# TEN

In the classroom, Jason hurried to his desk.

Miss Hershey held a hankie over her nose. "This room smells terrible," she said. "Who knows about this?"

Shawn said, "My *nose* does!"

The kids laughed. So did Miss Hershey. "My nose knows, too," she said.

In came the janitor with three big fans.

Jason and Dunkum opened all the windows.

Abby and Stacy made paper fans.

Then science class got started.

Miss Hershey called Dunkum's name. He did his taste test, but nobody could taste a thing. Everyone was holding their nose shut.

Dunkum explained, "This experiment proves my point. You can't taste, unless you can smell."

Abby and Stacy started coughing. Jason pretended to gag.

Dunkum's eyes watered. "Make it rain, Abby," he said. "Quick!"

"Yes," Miss Hershey said. "A good rain might clear the air."

Abby did her homemade rain project. With her teapot of hot water and soup dipper. But afterward, the smell was still strong.

Next, Stacy had the whole class cutting holes. "My project is called A Tight Squeeze," she said. "I will show how paper can stretch."

It was hard holding noses and handling scissors and paper. So Stacy showed the class how the cutting was done.

Then it was Eric's turn.

Some of the kids hissed. Jason started to boo.

"Class," Miss Hershey said. "That's *not* polite."

"But Eric put Limburger cheese in our sneakers," Stacy said.

Miss Hershey looked at Eric and frowned.

"I didn't do it," he said. "And I can prove it!"

Jason sat tall in his seat. He was worried.

Eric set up his science project. "This is a fingerprint experiment," he explained. "I made a record of fingerprints." He pointed to a grouping of prints mounted on poster board.

He showed the class how to make fin-

gerprints and how to dust for them.

"Now," he said. "I will prove that I didn't plant the Limburger cheese."

Jason leaned forward. He had to see this.

Eric held up a piece of cheese. "There's a thumbprint on this." He pinched his nose shut with his other hand. "You can't see it, but it's there."

Jason squirmed.

Eric continued. "The thumbprint on the cheese doesn't match mine," he said. "It doesn't match any of the prints I have."

Miss Hershey asked, "How many thumbprints did you take?"

Eric looked around the room. "I recorded everyone in the class." He looked at Jason. "Everyone, except one."

Jason squirmed even more.

Eric grinned. "I think I solved the stinky sneakers mystery."

Abby raised her hand. "Whose

63

thumbprint is missing?"

"Jason's," he said.

Jason stood up without being asked. He went to the front of the room.

All eyes were on him.

Eric opened his black ink pad. "Press your right thumb here," he said.

Jason pushed his thumb down. The pad felt gooey.

Eric pointed to a piece of paper. "Roll your thumb on this."

Jason obeyed. Then he lifted his thumb off the paper and looked down. Oval lines were there—where his thumb had been.

"Let's see if they match," Eric said. He compared Jason's thumbprint and the print on the cheese.

Miss Hershey watched closely.

All the kids stared.

Three fans hummed.

And Jason's heart thumped. Hard.

# ELEVEN

Miss Hershey stood up.

*Jason . . . Jason . . .* His name flew around the room.

"Quiet, please," Miss Hershey said.

Jason wanted to hide.

"I want you to stay after school," his teacher said. "Do you understand why?"

Jason nodded. "Yes, Miss Hershey."

After school, Jason wrote fifty times: *I will treat others with respect.*

Then Jason took the paper to Miss Hershey. "I have something to tell you," he said.

Miss Hershey looked up.

"I'm sorry about the stinky sneakers." Jason took a deep breath. "I just—" He paused.

"What is it, Jason?"

"Eric just made me so mad. I couldn't find my project this morning, and Eric made fun. He said I didn't even have one. But I *did*. A really super—" He stopped.

He didn't want to brag about the sprouts. Bragging had gotten him in big trouble.

Jason's voice grew soft. "I lost my science project."

"Can you find it by tomorrow?"

Jason felt better. "I hope so."

Miss Hershey smiled. "So do I."

Jason couldn't believe his ears. Tomorrow was the judging. If he found his sprouts, they might still win first place!

He ran all the way home.

★ ★ ★

At home, Jason searched for his sprouts.

He looked in the garage and on the back deck. He looked under the front porch. He even searched the attic.

But his project was missing. Maybe forever!

Then the doorbell rang.

Jason's mother called to him.

He sat on the beanbag in his room feeling sad. "Who is it?"

"Your friends are here to see you."

Jason sighed. He didn't move an inch.

Soon, he heard giggling. It was Stacy and Abby. He'd know their giggles anywhere.

Jason got up and scurried down the hall. The living room was full of kids—the Cul-de-sac Kids.

Stacy and Abby were still giggling. And now his mother was, too!

"What's so funny?" Jason asked.

Abby poked her hands in her pocket. "Oh, nothing."

Stacy tried to stop laughing.

Dunkum asked, "Where did you see your sprouts last?"

Jason thought. "On my windowsill," he said.

"*After* that," said Stacy.

Jason thought some more. "Beats me."

"Well, think!" Eric said.

Jason felt nervous. He looked around the room at his friends. "Do you know something I don't?" he asked.

All of them nodded.

Jason jumped up and down. "You've found my sprouts?"

Eric pointed to the kitchen. "Look! I can see them from here."

Jason whirled around. He stared straight ahead. Eric was right! The sprouts were in plain sight—on top of the refrigerator. Right where Stacy had put them.

Jason raced to the kitchen. He dragged a chair across the floor.

*Zoom!* He dashed back into the living room. His friends were smiling. Really smiling.

Jason stood there holding his sprouts. His stomach was in knots. "I'm sorry," he began. "I did a horrible thing . . . I mean about the cheese in your sneakers."

Dunkum went to stand beside Jason. "That's okay."

Eric frowned. "That's easy for *you* to say," he told Dunkum. "You don't have stinky sneakers!"

"*I* forgive Jason," Abby said. She came over and looked at his sprouts. "We stick together around here, remember?"

Shawn nodded. He ran around hugging all the kids.

Jason grinned.

# TWELVE

The next day, the Cul-de-sac Kids hurried to Blossom Hill School. Together.

When Miss Hershey saw Jason with his sprouts, she clapped.

"Look who found his project," Abby said.

Miss Hershey smelled the bright green alfalfa sprouts. "Mm-m. Could I pay you to grow some for me?" she asked Jason.

"Sounds good." Jason looked at Eric and Shawn. He looked at Abby and

71

Stacy. "I need to buy some new sneakers for my friends," he said.

Eric smiled. But not that sly smile.

Jason danced a jig to the science fair table. He put his sprouts on display.

Abby offered to water them. Eric straightened the plastic under the carpet.

Jason stepped back for a long look.

Then he knew. First place didn't matter anymore. Not really.

★ ★ ★

Later that day, the judges came to Miss Hershey's class. The first-place ribbon was big and blue. It had shiny gold letters on it.

The judge placed it next to Eric's fingerprint experiment. Eric had won. He deserved first place!

The class cheered. Especially Jason.

"Eric . . . Eric . . ." Jason started the chant.

The rest of the class joined in.

Eric's name flew all around the class-room.

And Jason was glad.

**THE CUL-DE-SAC KIDS SERIES**
**Don't miss #8!**

# PICKLE PIZZA

Eric Hagel wants to do something special for his German grandpa for Father's Day. The Cul-de-sac Kids have terrific gifts for their dads. But Eric can't think of anything to make. Besides that, he's broke!

Then Eric remembers something— his grandpa loves pickles. Pickles on eggs, pickles on cheese, pickles on everything. Eric has an idea. What about a pickle pizza?

Eric's plan falls apart when the girls in the cul-de-sac agree to a taste test. They gag and choke. Eric's pickle pizza is a flop.

Time has run out for Eric. *Now* what can he do?

# Also by Beverly Lewis

*The Beverly Lewis Amish Heritage Cookbook*

## GIRLS ONLY (GO!)
### Youth Fiction

| | |
|---|---|
| *Dreams on Ice* | *Follow the Dream* |
| *Only the Best* | *Better Than Best* |
| *A Perfect Match* | *Photo Perfect* |
| *Reach for the Stars* | *Star Status* |

## SUMMERHILL SECRETS
### Youth Fiction

| | |
|---|---|
| *Whispers Down the Lane* | *House of Secrets* |
| *Secret in the Willows* | *Echoes in the Wind* |
| *Catch a Falling Star* | *Hide Behind the Moon* |
| *Night of the Fireflies* | *Windows on the Hill* |
| *A Cry in the Dark* | *Shadows Beyond the Gate* |

## HOLLY'S HEART
### Youth Fiction

| | |
|---|---|
| *Best Friend, Worst Enemy* | *Straight-A Teacher* |
| *Secret Summer Dreams* | *No Guys Pact* |
| *Sealed With a Kiss* | *Little White Lies* |
| *The Trouble With Weddings* | *Freshman Frenzy* |
| *California Crazy* | *Mystery Letters* |
| *Second-Best Friend* | *Eight Is Enough* |
| *Good-Bye, Dressel Hills* | *It's a Girl Thing* |

## ABRAM'S DAUGHTERS
### Adult Fiction

| | |
|---|---|
| *The Covenant* | *The Sacrifice* |
| *The Betrayal* | *The Prodigal* |
| *The Revelation* | |

## THE HERITAGE OF LANCASTER COUNTY
### Adult Fiction

| | |
|---|---|
| *The Shunning* | *The Confession* |
| *The Reckoning* | |

## OTHER ADULT FICTION

*The Postcard* • *The Crossroad*
*The Redemption of Sarah Cain*
*October Song* • *Sanctuary\** • *The Sunroom*

*www.BeverlyLewis.com*

\*with David Lewis

# ABOUT THE AUTHOR

Beverly Lewis thinks Jason Birchall and all the Cul-de-sac Kids are super fun. She clearly remembers growing up on Ruby Street in her Pennsylvania home town. She and her younger sister played with the same group of friends year after year. Some of those childhood friends appear in her Cul-de-sac Kids series—disguised, of course!

Beverly thanks her niece, Amy, for the "super sprouts" idea in this story. (Yes, you really can grow alfalfa sprouts in a piece of carpet!)

If you love mystery and humor, be sure to read all the books in the Cul-de-sac Kids series.

# Girls Like You—
# PURSUING OLYMPIC DREAMS!

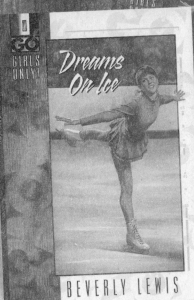

Don't miss the new series of books from Beverly Lewis called GIRLS ONLY (GO!). In this fun-loving series, you'll meet Olympic hopefuls like Livvy, Jenna, and Heather, girls training to compete in popular Olympic sports like figure-skating, gymnastics, and ice-dancing. Along the way, they tackle the same kinds of problems and tough choices you do—with friends and family, at school and at home. You'll love cheering on these likable girls as they face life's challenges and triumphs!

## GIRLS ONLY (GO!)

Dreams on Ice
Only the Best
A Perfect Match
Reach for the Stars

Follow the Dream
Better Than Best
Photo Perfect
Star Status

# POPULAR WITH SPORTS-MINDED GIRLS EVERYWHERE!

# THE LEADER IN CHRISTIAN FICTION!
## BETHANY HOUSE PUBLISHERS